JN058658

You Are Life

死を怖れない智慧

本田 つよし

You Are Life

Contents

Life

あなたはいのち
いのちとはあなた

いのちとは
あなたが所有するものではなく
あなたの存在そのもの

はるか昔からの
数えきれないいのちを
受け継ぐもの
それがあなた

いのちは途切れない
いのちは続いていく
だからあなたは
死を怖れなくてもいい

あなたはいのち
いのちとはあなた

You are life.
Life is you.

Life is not
What you have,
But what you are.

A continuation of
Countless lives
Since the beginningless past,
That's you.

Life never ceases.
Life continues.
So you don't have to be
Afraid of dying.

You are life.
Life is you.

The Sun And The Ocean

———

たとえ困難に会い
自分の道を見失っても
光は
あなたを照らしてくれる
その暗がりから
一歩踏み出す勇気があれば
いつでも太陽が
あなたに輝くように

あなたはそのままで
受け入れられる
その身を委ねれば
いつでも海があなたを
受け入れてくれるように

You will be illuminated
By the light
Even when you are in trouble
And lost sight of your path,
Like the sun will shine on you,
Whenever you have courage
To take one step
Out of the dark place.

You will be accepted
 Just as you are,
Like the ocean will accept you
Whenever you surrender yourself to it.

Acceptance

あなたがすべてを
受け入れた時
あなたのすべてが
受け入れられる

When you accept

Everything,

Your whole being

Will be accepted.

No Waste

すべてのことは
あなたをベストなあなたにするために
起こる

人生で起こることに
ムダなことは
ひとつもない

All things happens

To make you

The best of you.

There's no waste

That happens

 In your life.

As You Are

あなたは
そのままでいい

何が起こっても
抵抗する必要はないし
誰が背いても
非難する必要はない

あなたは
そのままでいい

It's just right

As you are.

No need to resist

Whatever happens to you.

No need to judge

Whoever goes against you.

It's just right

As you are.

Belief

あなたの信念には
あなたが考える以上に
あなたの人生を変える
力がある

それが環境の力より
はるかにパワフルだと
気づいた瞬間から
あなたの新しい人生が始まる

What you believe has

The more power

To transform your life

Than you think.

From the moment

You realize it is far more powerful

Than the power of your environment,

Your new life begins.

Belief II

自分を信じる人は
強い
自分より大きな何かを
信じる人は
もっと強い

Those who believe in themselves are

Strong.

Stronger than that are

Those who believe in

Something greater than themselves.

My Life

今はっきりとわかった
私の人生で起こったことは
すべて私を人として
ここにいさせるために起こった

それで十分ではないか？

I now truly realize.

Everything that happened

In my life is

To make me be here as a man.

That's good enough, isn't it ?

Role

天から
役目なしに
降ろされたものは
ひとつもないと言う

私の役目とは何か？

It is said

That there is no such thing

As being deposited from heaven

Without any role.

What is my role ?

You Are Loved

あなたは愛されている
不完全なままで
臆病で弱々しいままで
あなたは愛されている

これに気づいた時
本当の謙虚さと感謝が
あなたの中に生まれ
大いなる存在へと
導いてくれるのだ

You are loved.

As you are imperfect,

Coward and weak,

You are loved.

When you are aware of this,

True humility and gratitude

Are born within you,

Leading to

Something Great.

Buddha Nature

仏教を学ぶということは
自分自身の外側に
何か新しいものを
発見するというより
自分自身の内側に
眠っている何かを
呼び起こし
目覚めさせることなのだ

Learning Buddhism is

Recalling something sleeping

Inside yourself

And awakening it,

Rather than

Discovering

Something new

Outside yourself.

Understanding

広く知るより
深く知ることを
大切にしたい
さらに言えば
知ることより
わかることを
もっと
大切にしたいと思う

I would like to cherish

Profoundly knowing

Rather than

Extensively knowing.

Moreover,

Understanding

Rather than

Knowing.

Understanding II

いろいろなことを
知っているけれど
何ひとつ
わかっていない人

いろいろなことは
知らないけれど
ひとつのことを
しっかりと
わかっている人

どちらになりたいか？

The person

Who knows

Various things

But understand

Nothing.

The person

Who doesn't know

Various things

But surely understand

One thing.

Which do you want to become ?

Dharma

ダルマを求め続けなさい
たとえ回り道になろうとも
それはきっと
意味のある回り道

ダルマはけっして裏切らない
ダルマはあなたを
あなたにしているもの

ダルマを求め続けなさい

※ダルマ……宇宙の真理、法。

Keep seeking for Dharma.

Even if it be a detour,

It will surely be

A meaningful detour.

Dharma never betrays you.

Dharma is what makes you

What you are.

Keep seeking for Dharma.

Namu-Amida-Butsu

すべてはもう
あなたに与えられている

信心とは
この真実に気づくこと
そして念仏とは
この気づきから発する
感謝の表れ

南無阿弥陀仏

Everything is already
Given to you.

Entrusting heart is
To be aware of this truth
And nembutsu is
An expression of gratitude
From this realization.

Namu-Amida-Butsu.

Other Power (Tariki)

ただひたすら
阿弥陀様の力にすがりなさい

この言葉の
真の意味に気づいた時
あなたは本当に変わり
救われる

南無阿弥陀仏

料金受取人払郵便

小石川局承認

6163

差出有効期間
令和6年3月
31日まで
（期間後は切手をおはりください）

郵 便 は が き

112-8790

105

東京都文京区関口1-23-6
東洋出版 編集部 行

‖ءااااااءااااءاءااءاءاااااااااااااا

本のご注文はこのはがきをご利用ください

●ご注文の本は、小社が委託する本の宅配会社ブックサービス㈱より、1週間前後で
お届けいたします。代金は、お届けの際、下記金額をお支払いください。

お支払い金額＝税込価格＋手数料305円

●電話やFAXでもご注文を承ります。
電話 03-5261-1004　　FAX 03-5261-1002

ご注文の書名	税込価格	冊　数

● 本のお届け先　※下記のご連絡先と異なる場合にご記入ください。

ふりがな
お名前　　　　　　　　　　　　　　　　お電話番号

ご住所　〒　　　　　－

e-mail　　　　　　　　　　　　　　　@

ご記入いただいた個人情報は、お問い合わせへのお返事、ご注文の商品発送、新刊・企画などのご案内以外の目的には使用いたしません。

東洋出版の書籍をご購入いただき、誠にありがとうございます。
今後の出版活動の参考とさせていただきますので、アンケートにご協力
いただきますよう、お願い申し上げます。

● この本の書名
....

● この本は、何でお知りになりましたか?(複数回答可)
　1. 書店　2. 新聞広告(　　　　　新聞)　3. 書評・記事　4. 人の紹介
　5. 図書室・図書館　6. ウェブ・SNS　7. その他(　　　　　　　　　　)

● この本をご購入いただいた理由は何ですか?(複数回答可)
　1. テーマ・タイトル　2. 著者　3. 装丁　4. 広告・書評
　5. その他(　　　　　　　　　　　　　　　　　　　　　)

● 本書をお読みになったご感想をお書きください

● 今後読んでみたい書籍のテーマ・分野などありましたらお書きください

ご感想を匿名で書籍のPR等に使用させていただくことがございます。
ご了承いただけない場合は、右の□内に✓をご記入ください。　　□許可しない

※メッセージは、著者にお届けいたします。差し支えない範囲で下欄もご記入ください。

●ご職業　1.会社員　2.経営者　3.公務員　4.教育関係者　5.自営業　6.主婦
　　　　　7.学生　8.アルバイト　9.その他(　　　　　　　　　　)
●お住まいの地域

　　　都道府県　　　　　　　市町村区　男・女　年齢　　　歳

　　　　　　　　　　　　　　　　ご協力ありがとうございました。

Just single-mindedly

Rely on the Amida's power.

When you realize

The true meaning of this phrase,

You will be really

Transformed and saved.

Namu-Amida-Butsu.

Gratitude

生かされていることへの
感謝だけが
あなたを本当に幸せにする

感謝の無いところ
幸せも無い

生かされていることに
ただ感謝しなさい

Only gratitude

For being kept alive

Truly makes you happy.

No gratitude,

No happiness.

Just be grateful

For being kept alive.

Something Great

私を生かしている
サムシング・グレートの
そのはたらきに気づく時はいつも
不思議さと感謝を感じる

アミダにしろ、カミにしろ
確かにそれは存在しているのだ

南無阿弥陀仏

Whenever I'm aware of

The working of Something Great

That keeps me alive,

I feel wonder and gratitude.

Be it Amida or God,

I'm sure it does exist.

Namu-Amida-Butsu.

Proliferation

戯論に気をつけなさい

ネガティブな思いは
増殖しやすく
あなたを苦しめる

それが心というもの

いつでも心平和で
幸せでいたいなら
何よりも
戯論に気をつけなさい

Beware proliferation.

A negative thought
Is likely to be proliferated
And suffers you.

That's the way your mind is.

If you want to be at peace and happy
Anytime,
Beware proliferation
Above all.

Negative Spiral

あなたを
結局はダメにする
悪循環に
けっして巻き込まれないように

そのためには
気落ちするものから距離を置き
あなたを勇気づけるものと
いつも一緒にいることです

Never get involved in

Negative spiral

That ends up

Destroying you.

For that,

Keep away from discouraging things

And be with encouraging things

All the time.

The Path

仏道とは
知るためではなく
歩くためにある

The Buddhist path is
Not for knowing about
But for walking on.

Stillness

宇宙の声とは
「静寂」だと言う

心が完璧に
無になれば
その「声」が聴こえ
宇宙と
ひとつになれるはずだ

Voice of the universe

 Is said to be "stillness."

When you completely

Empty your mind,

You should be able to hear the "voice"

And become

One with the universe.

Warm Feelings

いつも私を
思わず涙させるもの
それは
誰かの温かな気持ちだ

The thing

That always makes me tears

Spontaneously is

Someone's warm feelings.

Way Of Life

誰かを利用して
自分を幸せにする人と
自分の幸せを後回しにしてでも
誰かを幸せにする人とでは
とてつもない違いが出るだろう

どちらの生き方を選ぶかは
あなた次第だ

There would be tremendous differences

Between those who make themselves happy

By using someone

And those who make someone happy

Even by putting off their own happiness.

It is up to you

Which way of life to take.

Respect

出会う人すべて
宅配便やコンビニのスタッフにでも
敬意を示しなさい

そうしなければ
今度はあなたが
尊敬されない人になる

Show respect to

Everyone you see

Even such as a courier, a store clerk.

If you do not,

You in turn end up

Not being respected.

Learning From Shohei And Sota

いつでも
謙虚で、思いやりの心を持ち
自分より他人のことを
優先しなさい

実は
それが自分を高めるための
最も上手く行くやり方なのです

Be humble,

Be compassionate,

And put others before you

All the time.

Actually,

That's the most effective way

To enhance yourself.

Not To Respond

誠意には
誠意で応え
悪意には
反応しない

それが
いつも平和で
幸せでいられる
やり方なのです

Have sincere response

To someone's sincerity

And do not respond

To any malice.

That's the way

To make you

Be at peace and happy

All the time.

Clean Mind

汚いものに
巻き込まれ
影響されたと感じたら
ただ気を取り直し
断固として心を清めなさい
そうすれば
悪はすべてあなたから逃げてゆく

忘れないで
あなたの心はもともと清い
そして清らかな心は
悪を寄せつけないのです

When you are involved

With dirty things

And feel influenced by them,

Just pull yourself together

And decisively cleanse your mind.

Then all evils

Will run away from you.

Remember,

Your mind is inherently clean,

And clean mind never attracts

Those evil things.

You And I

私のせいで
あなたが喜び
感謝する時はいつも
このままの私を
続けていく
気持ちにさせてくれる

あなたがいるから
私がいる

こちらこそありがとう

Whenever I find you

Be delighted and thankful,

Because of me,

It brings myself

To carry on

As I am.

I am here

Because you are here.

Thank YOU, too.

To Fully Live

すべての子供は
今ここで完全に生きたいと
思うものだ

でも年をとるにつれて
彼らは、つまり私たちは
あまりに多くのことに気を取られ
完全に生きることを忘れる

今ここに
ただ心を集めて
完全に生きよう

All children

Want to fully live

In the here and now.

But as they, we, get older,

We forget to fully live

With so many distractions

In our mind.

Just focus on

The here and now

And fully live.

Connected

だいじょうぶ

たとえ
誰ともつながっておらず
孤独だと感じていても
あなたは
大いなる存在とつながっていて
守られている

だいじょうぶ

It's just alright.

Even if you feel
Not connected to anyone
And lonely,
You are connected
To Something Great
And embraced.

It's just alright.

Amida And I

アミダとはいのち
私とはいのち
それゆえ
アミダと私は
ひとつ

南無阿弥陀仏

Amida is life.

I am life.

Therefore

Amida and I are

One.

Namu-Amida-Butsu.

My Creed

現在感謝

霊性満足

日々精進

蒔いたとおりに

花が咲く

Be grateful for this moment.

Be spiritually satisfied.

Devote yourself every day.

A flower blooms

As you sow its seed.

これで人生終わりだ——心の底からそう感じた日があった。その時私は、知らず知らずのうちに、親鸞の「歎異抄」の英訳文をただひた書き写していた。それから、ティク・ナット・ハンの『死もなく、怖れもなく』に出会い、第3詩集にも記したように、ケネス田中先生の『真宗入門』にたどり着いた。第4詩集となる本作品は、大いなる「いのち」の不思議への感謝のしるしです。

どうか、みなさまが、心平和で幸せでありますように。
南無阿弥陀仏。

本田つよし

This is the end of my life —there was a day when I felt this way from the bottom of my heart. At that time, unknowingly, I single-mindedly transcribed the English translation of Shinran's "*Tannisho*."

Thereafter, I encountered "*No Death, No Fear*" by Thich Nhat Hanh, and got to "*Ocean*" by Kenneth Tanaka sensei, as I mentioned in my third anthology. This work, my fourth, is an expression of gratitude to the mystery of great "Life."

May you all be at peace and happy.
Namu-Amida-Butsu.

HONDA Tsuyoshi

Recommended books

『歎異抄をひらく』高森顕徹　１万年堂出版

"UNLOCKING TANNISHO" Kentetsu Takamori.
Ichimannendo Publishing

『死もなく、怖れもなく』ティク・ナット・ハン　春秋社

"NO DEATH, NO FEAR" Thich Nhat Hanh. RIVERHEAD BOOKS

『真宗入門』ケネス・タナカ　法蔵館

"Ocean" Kenneth K. Tanaka. WisdomOcean Publications

HONDA Tsuyoshi

本田つよし

Profile

プロフィール

Born in Kumamoto Prefecture. Graduated from Waseda University.

熊本県生まれ。早稲田大学第一文学部英文学科卒業。

Weblog "English for Happiness"　ブログ「しあわせになる英語」

https://www.englishforhappiness.com/

X (formerly Twitter)

https://twitter.com/englishforhapp

A member of the Steering Committee of "Sangha for Studying and Practicing
Buddhism Through Basic English"

「仏教を初歩英語で学び実践するサンガの会」運営委員

You Are Life
死を怖れない智慧

発行日　　2024 年 5 月 21 日　第 1 刷発行

著者　　　本田 つよし（ほんだ・つよし）

発行者　　田辺修三
発行所　　東洋出版株式会社
　　　　　〒 112-0014　東京都文京区関口 1-23-6
　　　　　電話　03-5261-1004（代）　振替　00110-2-175030
　　　　　http://www.toyo-shuppan.com/

印刷・製本　日本ハイコム株式会社

許可なく複製転載すること、または部分的にもコピーすることを禁じます。
乱丁・落丁の場合は、ご面倒ですが、小社までご送付下さい。
送料小社負担にてお取り替えいたします。

© Tsuyoshi Honda 2024, Printed in Japan

ISBN 978-4-8096-8707-5　定価はカバーに表示してあります

ISO14001 取得工場で印刷しました